In Loving Memory

Greyson T. Allen

AMAZING AUNT AGATHA

First Steck-Vaughn Edition 1992

Copyright © 1990 American Teacher Publications

Published by Steck-Vaughn Company

Library of Congress number: 90-8016

Library of Congress Cataloging in Publication Data.

Samton, Sheila White.
  Amazing Aunt Agatha / by Sheila Samton; illustrated by Yvette Banek.

  (Ready-set-read)
  Summary: An adventurous African-American woman and her nephew make their way through alphabet accomplishments from Amazing audiences to Zipping zebras.
  [1. Afro-Americans—Fiction. 2. Alphabet.] I. Banek, Yvette Santiago, ill. II. Title. III. Series.
PZ7.S185Am 1990   [E]—dc20/   90-8016

ISBN 0-8172-3575-2   hardcover library binding

ISBN 0-8114-6737-6   softcover binding

2 3 4 5 6 7 8 9 0   96 95 94 93 92

AMAZING AUNT AGATHA

by Sheila Samton
illustrated by Yvette Banek

STECK-VAUGHN
C O M P A N Y
A Subsidiary of National Education Corporation

A   **a**

Andrew's **A**unt **A**gatha
Amazes **a**udiences,

4

B

b

Builds **b**oats,

C **c**

Collects clocks,

Draws **d**inosaurs,

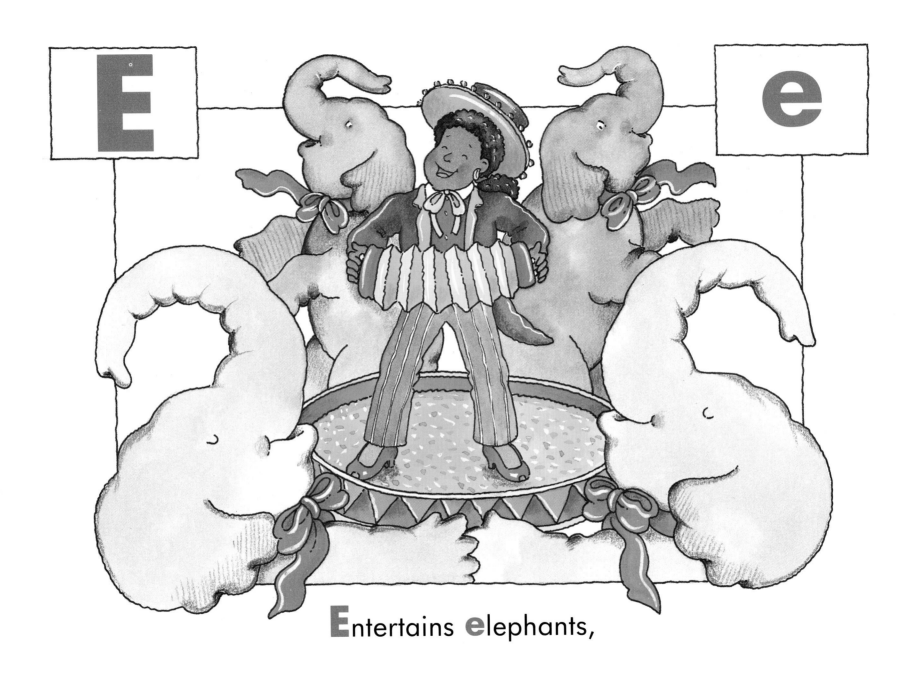

E **e**

Entertains **e**lephants,

F **f**

Fries frankfurters,

G **g** **H** **h**

Greets **g**orillas,   **H**elps **h**ippos,

Inspects igloos,

Juggles jellybeans,

K

k

Kisses **k**ittens,

L **l**

Lifts **l**ions,

M **m** **N** **n**

Makes **m**asks, **N**ibbles **n**oodles,

14

O **o** **P** **p**

Outswims **o**ctopuses,

Pets **p**anthers,

15

Q **q**

Quiets **q**uarrels,

R **r**

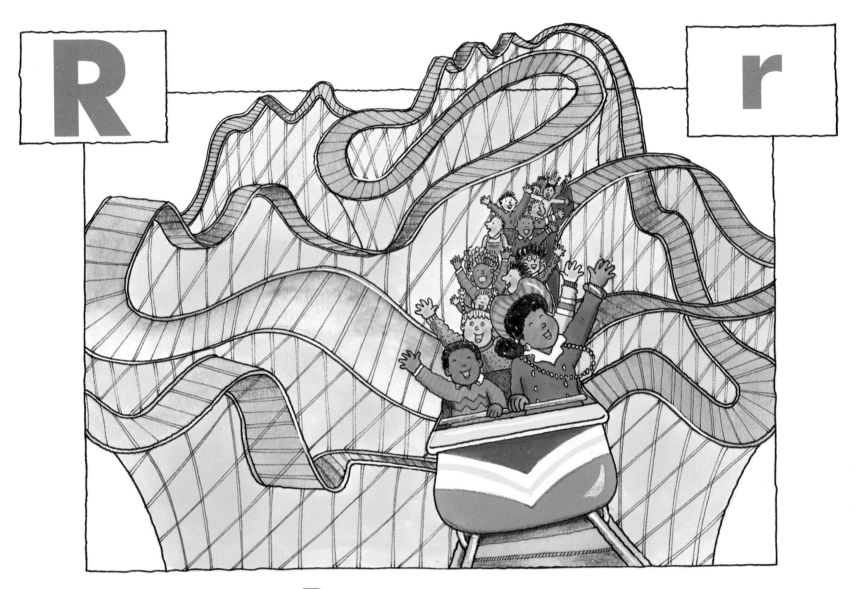

Rides **r**ollercoasters,

17

S s T t

Serenades **S**ea **S**erpents,   **T**racks **t**arantulas,

U u V v

Understands **u**nicorns,

Visits **v**olcanoes,

Washes **w**easels,

X-rays **x**ylophones,

Y y Z z

Yells **y**ahoo,   **Z**ips **z**ebras,

ABCDEFGH
abcdefghi

and **a**bsolutely **a**dores **A**ndrew!

22

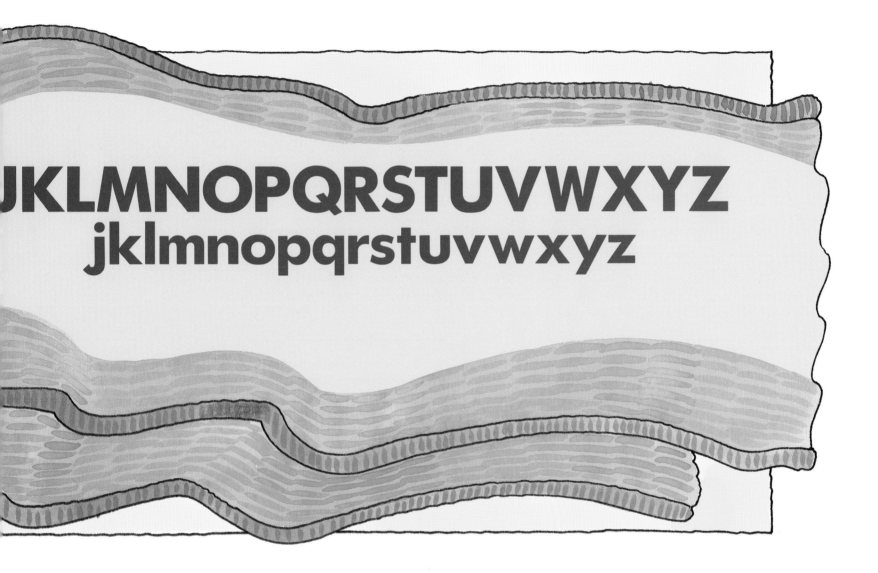

JKLMNOPQRSTUVWXYZ

jklmnopqrstuvwxyz

Sharing the Joy of Reading

Reading a book aloud to your child is just one way you can help your child experience the joy of reading. Now that you and your child have shared **Amazing Aunt Agatha,** you can help your child begin to think and react as a reader by encouraging him or her to:

- Retell or reread the story with you, looking and listening for the repetition of specific letters, sounds, words, or phrases.

- Make a picture of a favorite character, event, or key concept from this book.

- Talk about his or her own ideas or feelings about the characters in this book and other things that the characters might do.

Here is an activity that you can do together to help extend your child's appreciation of this book: You and your child can talk about a favorite relative or friend. What does this person like to do that is special? What words would you use to describe this person? Your child can give examples or draw a picture of himself or herself doing something special with this person.